PLATFORM PAPERS

QUARTERLY ESSAYS ON THE PERFORMING ARTS FROM CURRENCY HOUSE

No. 39
May 2014

Platform Papers Partners

We acknowledge with gratitude our Partners in continuing support of Platform Papers and its mission to widen understanding of performing arts practice and encourage change when it is needed:

Gillian Appleton
Anita Luca Belgiorno Nettis Foundation
Jane Bridge
Katharine Brisbane, AM
Elizabeth Butcher, AM
Peter Cooke, OAM
Rowena Cowley and Dr Richard Letts, AM
Ian Enright
Larry Galbraith
Tony Grierson
Gail Hambly
Wayne Harrison, AM
Peter Lee
Roderick H. McGeoch, AO
Harold Mitchell, AC, AO
Joanna Murray-Smith
Martin Portus
Positive Solutions
Seaborn Broughton Walford Foundation
Professor Di Yerbury, AM

To them and to all subscribers and Friends of Currency House we extend our grateful thanks.

Contents

1 THE RETREAT OF OUR NATIONAL DRAMA
JULIAN MEYRICK

81 Readers' Forum
Michael Hooper on Peter Tregear's *Enlightenment or Entitlement: Rethinking tertiary music education* (Platform Papers 38)

AVAILABILITY Platform Papers, quarterly essays on the performing arts, is published every February, May, August and November and is available through bookshops, by subscription or online. For details see our website at www.currencyhouse.org.au.

LETTERS Currency House invites readers to submit letters of 400–1,000 words in response to the essays. Letters should be emailed to the Editor at info@currencyhouse.org.au or posted to Currency House at PO Box 2270, Strawberry Hills, NSW 2012, Australia. To be considered for the next issue, the letters must be received by 15 June.

The RETREAT of OUR NATIONAL DRAMA

JULIAN MEYRICK

About the Author

Julian Meyrick is Professor of Creative Arts at Flinders University, Artistic Counsel for the State Theatre Company of South Australia and an Honorary Associate at La Trobe University. From 1989 to 1998 he was Artistic Director of kickhouse theatre and from 2002 to 2007 Associate Director and Literary Advisor at Melbourne Theatre Company. He was a founder member and Deputy Chair of Playwriting Australia 2004–09, and a member of the Federal Government's Creative Australia Advisory Group 2008–10. He is the director of many award-winning theatre productions, most recently *Angela's Kitchen*, that he co-authored with Paul Capsis, and which attracted the 2012 Helpmann Award for best Australian work. He was also director of the inaugural production of *Who's Afraid of the Working Class?* and winner of the 1998 Green Room Award for best director on the Fringe. Before entering the theatre he studied economics and politics, later returning to university to become a historian with an interest in quantitative and qualitative research methodologies. He has published histories of the Nimrod Theatre and the Melbourne Theatre Company, Platform Paper No.3 (2005) and numerous articles on Australian theatre, cultural policy and contemporary dramaturgy. He is currently part of a cultural value research team at Flinders University investigating new ways of assessing the public benefit of cultural organisations and events.

Acknowledgements

Many people have contributed to the research and writing of this essay. I would particularly like to thank Dr Jonathan Bollen for his exhaustive mining of the AusStage data base and his many astute comments on the limits of statistical inference in relation to repertoire data; and Jenny Fewster for showing me the capacities of this important on-line resource, and hunting down facts and figures at short notice. I am also grateful to May-Brit Akerholt and Terence Crawford who, over a six-month period, exchanged lengthy emails on the nature of classic adaptations and the adaptation process. Alas, only a small proportion of this enlightening conversation has found its way into these pages. I thank my colleagues in the School of Humanities at Flinders University, who amidst their own too-busy lives, are invariably supportive of my projects. The time and resources that Professors Richard Maltby and Diana Glenn allowed me to devote to this essay have been key to its delivery.

I would like to thank all the artists, particularly playwrights, but by no means only playwrights, who spoke to me about the role and impact of classic adaptations in the repertoire today. In every instance, they expressed subtle views and feelings. It was this complexity of response that persuaded me something important was going on. Finally, I am grateful to Katharine Brisbane and Currency House for giving me an opportunity, a second time, to comment on a matter that affects Australian theatre in a signal way.

The 2013 Adaptation Debate

- *May 25-26.* Rosemary Neill writes a cover article for the *Weekend Australian*, 'Hooked on Classics', arguing that adaptations of classic plays dominate the Australian mainstream repertoire and wondering if 'this is a sign of the bankruptcy of original ideas or [...] a confident fresh approach to great works of drama?' A number of artists comment, including director Simon Stone who defends his free approach to adaptation saying 'authorship only became sacrosanct when Walt Disney invented copyright [...] At the end of the day it's an actor and an audience, not a writer and an audience'. The *Australian* announces 'a war of words has erupted over the boom in updated classics sweeping Australia'.
- *May 28.* A follow-up article, 'The Local Voices Being Swept off the Stage', solicits more opinions. Playwright Andrew Bovell comments, 'Nothing will stifle the creativity of Australian playwrights more than the belief that our best is not good enough, while the rewriting of European plays comes to pass as an Australian theatre'. Stone makes the claim that 'more often than not [Australian playwrights] write bad plays'.
- *May 30.* Ralph Myers, artistic director of Belvoir, argues the adaptation debate is 'creat[ing] a false distinction between playwrights and the people who

make theatre [...] What Neill has actually identified is not a battle between playwrights and directors but a generational conflict. The three playwrights she quotes [...] David Williamson, Patricia Cornelius and Andrew Bovell [...] are finding themselves side-lined by a new generation of theatre-makers.'

- *3 June.* The Australian Writers Guild calls for 'respect for writers and new Australian work'. Executive director Jacqueline Elaine argues that 'if writers are writing for stage and screen it is because they are seeking the alchemy of successful collaboration [...] A true collaboration is one in which the writers should be acknowledged, indeed acclaimed. Ideas are easy. Turning them into compelling scripts is really bloody hard. That's what good writers do.'
- *20 June.* Critic Jane Howard reviews Belvoir's production of *Angels in America* and argues 'I couldn't help but feel that [the production] was undeniably Australian. The text, the setting and the accents were all American [...] but the production felt like a new Australian work... Our focus so often seems to be on the script. [But] the world of a play is made up by so many people beyond the writers—if, indeed, there is a writer involved at all.'
- *21 June.* Playwright Peter Fleming rebuts Myer's comments, calling them 'rude, offensive and ageist'. 'If we take Myers' argument to its logical conclusion, why stop at reworking plays from a few decades ago? [...] Let's follow the Down with Copyright banner to works of last year or last week'.
- *21 June.* Aubrey Mellor, former artistic director of Playbox Theatre, responds to Neill commenting, 'adaptation versus interpretation is an age-old issue. Personally,

I love adaptations and often prefer them to the original. However, there comes a point where a line is crossed and when [that happens] the work should be retitled.'

- *22 June.* David Berthold, artistic director of La Boite, blogs that 'The framing of the debate has often been poor: auteur vs author, director vs playwright, adaptations vs new plays, Simon Stone vs Australian playwrights, Ralph Myers vs the baby boomers. The misleading binaries have not diminished passions. One wonders what truly lurks below.'
- *3 July.* Playwright Lachlan Philpott takes his name off a Perth Theatre Company's production of *AlieNation,* saying, 'I would like to acknowledge the people who bravely shared their stories and the actors and creative artists who contributed to this work in good faith. However, the outcome of this production does not reflect my original, scripted or communicated intentions as a playwright.' PTC puts out a press release saying it 'strongly disagrees' with Philpott's statements.
- *1 August.* Alison Croggon contributes a statistics-based article, assisted by Jane Howard, in response to 'a series of inflammatory articles [presenting] playwrights [as] a threatened species'. Commenting that 'this is a debate marked by polarised and often vitriolic language' she compares the repertoires of Australia's major theatre companies in 2013 and 2003. 'Our main stages produced no fewer Australian plays than they did in 2003. But these bald stats nevertheless reveal a massive change in theatrical practice. The growth in AMPAG productions is driven by new Australian work […] of a completely new category, devised theatre, as well as adaptations of novels, films or plays by Australian

artists.' She concludes 'it's clear that some things can definitely be improved for writers in our theatre, but neither is the situation as dire as it is commonly painted.' A lengthy on-line discussion takes place between Croggon and Neill about statistical categories, and what counts and doesn't count as an 'Australian play'.

- *5 August.* Tim Roseman, artistic director of Playwriting Australia, laments the lack of diversity in the repertoire of the major companies, arguing 'we're just not showing a representative range of Australian voices, culture and traditions on our main stages. Despite indigenous Australians and those from a culturally diverse background [...[making up 34% of the population, last year only 13% of plays produced were by writers reflecting that.'
- *9 August.* Reflecting on his remark that 'more often than not, [Australian playwrights] write bad plays, Simon Stone comments ruefully, 'that interview was a really unfortunate experience. I said it was easier to use a classic play to talk about now, because you have a form already there. Theatre companies want a surface success, and classics are easier to do, even if they are responding to our time and place in a less deep and accurate way. You don't have to develop the text for four or five years, as you do with a new play. I was actually trying to be self-effacing'.

INTRODUCTION

'Genius is that which will not adapt.'
Henry Miller

This essay discusses the on-going furore over adaptations of classic plays in Australian theatre that erupted, seemingly out of nowhere, in the media last year. Despite a vociferous exchange of views, it is not entirely clear what constitutes an adaptation, or why this approach to textual drama should provoke such strong reactions. What on earth is going on?

I will try to define the term and clarify the context of its application today. This exercise in intellectual hygiene, however, is unlikely to mollify the debate's combatants, angry and perplexed on the one hand, blithe and overruling on the other. For this is not in the end an argument about plays, old or new. It is about the expectations Australian artists and audiences have of one another, and Australian artists have of themselves. These are to some extent historically determined and while practitioners are free to imagine impossible theatres, it is the possible ones that find favour and funding. Because the play script is for many companies an Archimedean point in the theatre-making process its choice is significant. A season of plays reflects a stance by artists towards the world. Audiences may confirm this stance or not, but within limits. However sensitive they claim to be to patron demand, artists still use their specialised knowledge to make informed judgements about the repertoire. Not only the plays selected for production but the *type* of plays selected is of intense interest. The invisible categories of sense (the 'slots') that hover over individual scripts and push them forward as potential stage experiences, shape—or break—hopes and careers.

The essay has three parts to it. The first is historical and discusses the role of the 'adaptive mentality' in Australian theatre as an evolving industrial fact. The second is analytical and is a brief love letter to play scripts from a director who has spent his life trying to understand their enigmatic power. The third part is testimony, part of my own story of developing and staging new drama and watching other artists engage in the same task. This takes in my time as associate director and literary adviser at Melbourne Theatre Company setting up a nascent play development program, Hard Lines, as well as working with smaller companies and independently. Taken together, the three sections form both an explanation and an argument. They explore what adaptations are and provide a sense of when their programming is legitimate.

That adaptations have an illegitimate side is not provable in a scientific sense. For a country like Australia, however, with a fragile cultural ecology and a history of colonial domination, setting limits on foreign imports is both wise and necessary. But this negative critical point is far, far less important than the positive argument that *it is time for Australians to acknowledge that a fully functioning national drama is not a gold-taps luxury but a vital component of civic maturation.*

For all the much-vaunted advances in mixed-media performance there is nothing like *saying it.* Words retain their dominant hold over our fund of knowledge and experience. Indeed, the core of the adaptations issue is a dispute about which words on our stages we should be hearing. And while there is enjoyment and edification to be had from the historical repertoire, our relationship with the past makes sense only in terms of our relationship with the present. New play development puts the canon to the question and provides a standpoint from which to view it as something more than a parade of opportunistic product.

This might not be immediately obvious. When a show in the theatre 'works' and fills us with a sense of energised participation, why hanker for something more? For something that doesn't 'work' or not in the same way? Why pursue a corpus of plays that can be brought into being only with difficulty, uncertainty and effort, rather than identifying 'the best' drama has to offer and sticking with that?

Because there comes a time in the life of a people, as there does in an individual, when articulating a response to a changing world becomes more pressing than a need for assured success. Drama is an incomparable way of freighting life experience. Drama—and I include film, television and digital media—assays what

Lionel Trilling called a nation's 'secret life'.[11] German Expressionism after World War I, British Absurdism in the 1950s, and New Wave theatre in Australia in the 1970s, all made subcutaneous thoughts and feelings available in stage form. Drama is an unparalleled method of account, a trackless ship of the imagination. It is courtroom, marketplace, street corner, bedchamber, battlefield, dreamscape, garden of Eden, fiery hell; a furious, funny, prescient means of telling ourselves things we don't want to know, but need to know.

Drama's benefits are thus considerable and extend well beyond the theatre, an art form most Australians regard as elite, antique or affected. Nevertheless the live stage remains drama's proving ground. When David Hare's *Stuff Happens* premiered at London's National Theatre in 2005, so great was the shock at seeing George Bush portrayed as a canny leader, and Tony Blair as a fool, that it changed perceptions of the second Iraq war and probably UK public policy as well. The responses to Caryl Churchill's *Seven Jewish Children*, Tony Kushner's *Angels in America* and Kate Grenville's *Secret River* (an adaptation of the legitimate sort), were similarly seismic, showing the considerable power live drama continues to wield. To achieve these benefits requires more than professional skill, of however high an order. It requires intellectual and emotional engagement of the deepest and most personal kind. It requires investigation into the intentions and values of a play script to find out not only whether it 'works' but why it exists in the first place, what it is trying to say or show. Without this we are, though we may not realise it, staging the same play over and over again, reducing the diverse contours of a fervent medium down to our own quotidian concerns. At some point we need to depart from known outcomes and strike out on our own. Only in this way can we participate in drama's journey of discovery, as a culture seeking to contribute to its myriad means of expression. However much we admire *the old* we have to create *the new* to appreciate the old as it was when first created.

Here a different risk profile comes into view. A balance between old and new in the repertoire is clearly a sensible thing, given that these are not absolute qualities—that there is a lot of the old in the new, and something new in every production of the old. But as types of activity, as arcs of commitment, they are poles apart. For the new is wholly unknown and the joy and terror that results from this induces a singular appreciation of theatre's horizons. This is a key point. A commitment to a national drama is not just about the results. It is about the altered mind-set that comes when our own imagination is set free to soar. Then *everything* is changed, not only the kinds of plays selected but the means mobilized to make those selections, and the values used to judge the results. Just as in life we feel differently driving through countryside we have explored on foot, so creating our own drama enriches the spirit of an entire theatre culture.

If ever an example existed of this, it is Australia. For upwards of sixty years after federation the country struggled with the idea of a national drama, failing to appreciate its signal qualities as a change agent. The adaptation debate reflects these historical fears—that the country could slide back into a branch town mentality, losing not simply its 'stories' but its capacity to frame reality according to its own view of life.

Why should playwrights have a leading role in all this? In many ways they don't. But writing does. It is the function, not the personalities, that matters and part of my argument will be that while writers aren't special people they are charged with an especially demanding task and this deserves our recognition and support, even as we acknowledge other artists and their important roles. This is different from saying that playwrights should be at the apex of theatre or have the final say in all aspects of production or that all theatre should be created in the same way. This is patently false, and today's industry is full of writers in varied work situations—cooperative, collaborative and cross-art form—and projects re-routing the literary component of the theatre-making processes.

But this is not a recent occurrence. Different ways of working have been a reality in theatre for as long as theatre has been a reality. Diversity does not need to be defended. Rather the problems facing particular approaches need to be better understood. Playwriting is an intense expression of certain challenges and capacities without which a crucial articulation of the dramatic imagination cannot take place. It is a concentrated form of the 'encounter with the new', and I return to my point about language. Language *says things*, committing those who open their mouths to its specific propositions. It can be ambiguous, poetic, allusive, elliptical. But it can also array to precise effect. We know things in drama with clarity and force because they are expressed in words and their devastating twin, silence. This makes drama a serious public art form, a shaper of manners and morals, a way a society talks to itself in the night, and beyond the night.

—

What is 'adaptation'? The *Oxford English Dictionary* gives this definition: 'the action or process of fitting or suiting one thing to another [...] modification to fit a new use'. Closer to home, the Australian journalist Matthew Westwood writing in the wake of Melbourne Theatre Company's 2012 *Queen Lear*—an adaptation that didn't 'work'[2]—observed:

> *adaptation satisfies a particular strain of curiosity for theatregoers. An original play can be judged only on its own terms. An adaptation, good or bad, will almost invariably be judged against the original [...] If one accepts adaptation is the animating force of the arts, then attempts to stifle it are anathema to creativity [...] It is by standing on the shoulders of giants that artists create something new'.*[3]

This touches on the central issue. The adaptations

debate is not an argument about recovering the past for its own sake but about a relationship of use between 'source' and 'target' textual artefacts. Is this relationship really the animating force of the arts? Even if it isn't, for a medium in which play scripts have accrued in significant numbers it is an important one. Westwood refers to the self-consciousness of the connection, and here he is surely right again. The adaptations that stalk the boards today have a knowing relationship with their source texts, and audiences participate in this and glean pleasure from it: feel that they, too, are standing on the shoulders of giants.

Four modes of theatrical adaptation are in common use today. First, there are medium-to-medium adaptations, where a book, poem or film script is turned into a stage play. The 2013 Helpmann Award winner *Secret River,* originally a novel by Kate Grenville, is a good example. Second, there are language-to-language adaptations where a foreign source text is translated into a domestic target language. Ibsen, Strindberg, Chekhov and Brecht are examples of playwrights regularly translated into English where Westwood's sense of an original applies, though not in a uniform way. Third, there are period-to-period adaptations, where the process of 'suiting' is one of historical mediation. Shakespeare is a case in point. The speeches on kingship that punctuate *Richard II* are impenetrable for modern audiences, so they are often amended or left out, as are words that no longer have currency ('yarely', 'anters', 'brach' etc.). Finally, there is a catch-all category of cultural transposition, where something 'other' is recoded into a more familiar register. This applies to contemporary versions of US classics, like Benedict Andrews' 2007 production of Edward Albee's *Who's Afraid of Virginia Woolf?* that stripped it of period features, or Simon Stone's 2012 production of Arthur Miller's *Death of a Salesman* which changed the ending of the story. This elasticity is reflected in the nomenclature accompanying a diversity of production approach: 'based on', 'a version of', 'after' etc. Instead of thinking of the adaptations category as a box into which plays can be dropped like tennis balls it is better to posit a spectrum of effort, with tight-fit, true-to-period revivals at one end and radical, left-of-field re-imaginings at the other. That many of these are associated with their directors' hints at the power relations underlying apparently literary choices. If, as some argue, the playwright is downgraded in the process of adaptation, it is clear enough who has benefitted. While it can be handled collaboratively, adaptation is often channelled through a narrow set of roles chief of which is that of the director.

What are the values governing this industry of reclamation? Academic scholarship has produced numerous books on the politics of translation and adaptation. Lawrence Venuti and Linda Hutcheon are two authors who have written at length on the issue. Venuti's *The Translator's Invisibility* notes that, 'for the most part, English-language translators [...] let their choice of foreign texts and their development of translation strategies conform to dominant cultural values in English'.[4]

Hutcheon is more upbeat. In *A Theory of Adaptation* she observes,

> *the 'success' of an adaptation today in the age of transmedia can no longer be determined in relation to its proximity to [an] 'original'[...] Perhaps it is time to look instead to popularity, persistence, [...] diversity and extent of dissemination [...] This is how biology thinks about adaptation: in terms of successful replication and change'.*[5]

Quite obviously this kind of discourse does not guide practitioners when they take out their knife and fork and attack their stock of old plays. The uptick in classic adaptations has less to do with the nuances of intercultural scholarship than with the industry's own needs and desires. Which is not to say it is without intellectual motivation, only that its drivers are proximate ones. Despite its internationalist flavour, the recourse to adaptation in the repertoire is a very Australian thing.

Some numbers

Before examining why this is so, however, it is helpful to look at the numbers. Repertoire statistics usually inform arguments rather than settle them. Difficulties arise from the fact that the data populations are usually small and lack an informing context. Size of venue, length of run, the nature of transfers or tours, and the profile of associated artists are all factors determining a show's significance that repertoire categories do not capture. If we wanted to be completely accurate, we would establish an index to weight these factors so that proper comparison could be made. But this would be controversial since a show's merit might have little to do with its external traits and no objective measure of intrinsic quality currently exists.

Problems also arise from definitions. Categories are a two-dimensional way of representing three-dimensional experience. What is or is not a 'classic' or 'Australian' or 'new' is, again, a controversial matter and unitizing the difficulty hides it behind a façade of pseudo-objectivity. 'I come from the position', a colleague said to me recently, 'that figures are always dodgy'. A number is a descriptive contraction, a reduction of feature to aggregate mark. It is not that numbers can be made to say anything; but in an art form where unique experience is the point of the craft, statistical generalisations are weak reflections of the empirical ground from which they are drawn.

These caveats acknowledged, Table 1 presents the aggregated repertoire percentages of nine companies from 1987 to 2013. It includes four state theatres: Sydney Theatre Company (STC), Melbourne Theatre Company (MTC), South Australian State Theatre Company (SASTC) and Queensland Theatre Company (QTC); one quasi-state theatre (Black Swan in Perth) and four second-tier theatres, Belvoir (in Sydney), Playbox/Malthouse (in Melbourne), Brink (in Adelaide) and La Boite (in Brisbane). This furnishes a dataset of

2,103 distinct production events and permits some basic inferences to be drawn. Shows are broken down into five categories: *overseas recent, overseas classics, Australian classics, Australian recent and Australian new (premieres)*.[6] The two classics categories include play scripts more than fifteen years old, of either Australian or overseas origin, and adapted source texts of like age.[7]

Table 1: All Companies 1987–2013

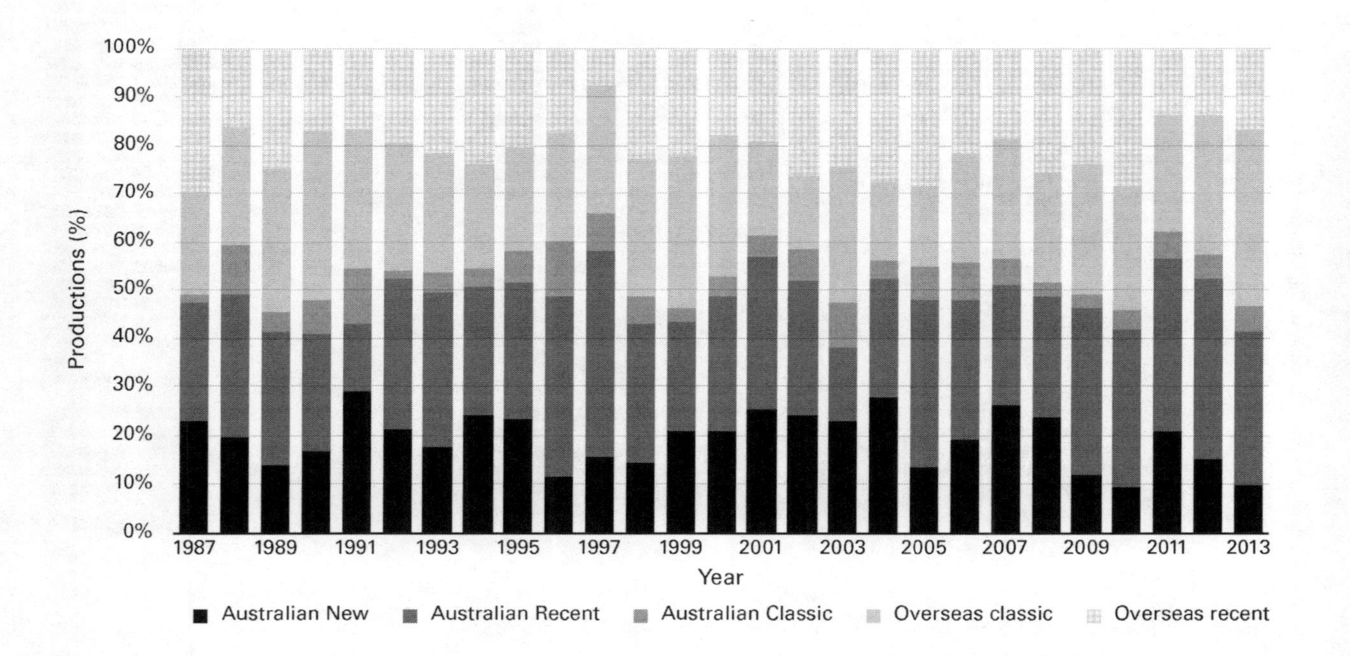

Table 2: Sydney Theatre Company, 1987–2013

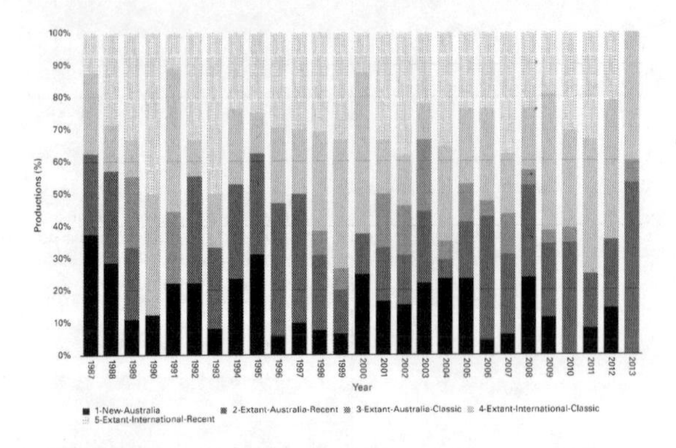

Table 3: Melbourne Theatre Company, 1987–2013

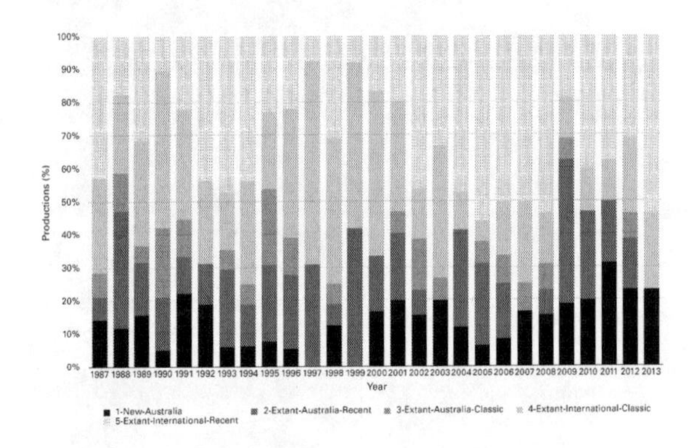

Table 4: Belvoir Theatre, 1987–2013

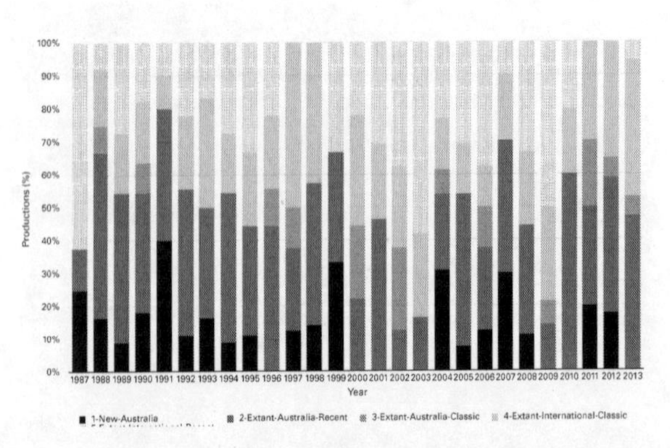

Table 5: Playbox/Malthouse, 1987–2013

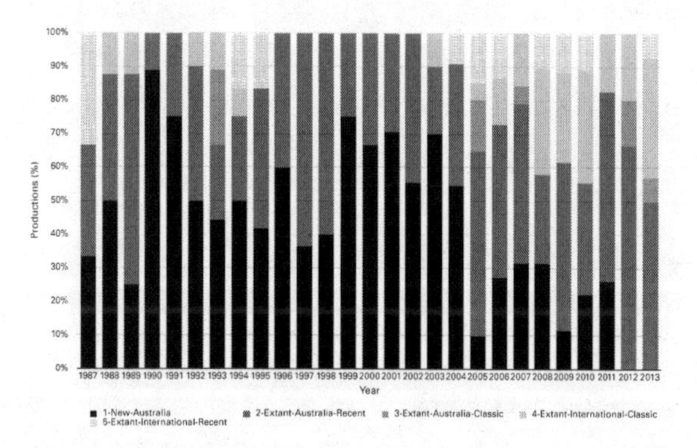

These figures are taken from the AusStage database, the most extensive collection of theatre information available. Its broad sweep, coupled with the complex history of many plays, means that trait capture is never perfect. Table 1 is best viewed, therefore, as a *clash between the bottom three data series and the upper two.* This furnishes a broad division between Australian and overseas work and a first observation: that Australian drama of one kind or another fills 45% to 65% of the repertoire, and that its fate is a serious matter. This is especially true for second-tier theatres (average 70% of repertoire), but sufficiently true for state theatres (average 36%). Australian drama is not a question of faith, hope and charity, as in the past. It is core to the business of our theatre sector, a major output and brand identifier.

The areas swept out by the different categories change over time, but not by much. For both state and second-tier theatres there is a drop in the programming of Australian drama after peaks in the 2000s. However, small shifts in absolute numbers can produce large-looking shifts in percentages, so in general the graphs support Alison Croggon's claim that the proportion of Australian vs. overseas work is the same over the period.[8] There is no way of knowing, though, at what level plays are being programmed, (whether they are housed in studio rather than mainstage seasons). For this, we have to turn to the individual companies and their separate contexts.

Tables 2 to 5 present percentage graphs for STC, MTC, Belvoir and Playbox/Malthouse. The STC shows a rise in classic drama after 2008, sometimes at the expense of Australian, sometimes overseas, work. These peaks are cyclical over the period, exemplified by the Actors Company (2005–07) whose mini-repertoire of ten plays contains six classics and thee new Australian plays (one based on Ovid's *Metamorphosis).* High-profile tours of *Hedda Gabler, A Streetcar Named Desire* and *Big and Little,* which featured Cate Blanchett, add to the picture of a company with a historically strong commitment to classic drama whose recent preferences reflect the actor-focus of its operation and the presence of two notable adaptors on staff (Andrew Upton and Tom Wright). The MTC, by contrast, shows a trend away from classics, especially after 2004. The gainer is overseas drama rather than Australian plays, so that in respect of the latter category the STC fares better. This might indicate the presence of a studio program, however, something the MTC acquires in 2008, after which its percentage of Australian drama improves.

Overall, the numbers suggest a company for whom 'new' rather than 'old' work dominates, of whatever origin, a trait possibly attributable to Simon Phillips, artistic director 1999–2011, known for his productions of large-scale musicals and contemporary works.

Belvoir's graph tells yet another story, this time of both classics *and* Australian drama increasing at the expense of overseas work. The proportion of the last declines significantly when Ralph Myers replaces Neil Armfield as artistic director in 2010. Only with the Playbox/Malthouse graph do we see classics rapidly increase off a very small base. This happens after 2005, with the change in artistic director from Aubrey Mellor to Michael Kantor, and a consequent rebranding of the company. What had been a near-exclusive commitment to Australian drama is reduced, with classics jumping as high as 30% of program thereafter. Here is an unabashed change in direction but the story is not typical. There is no typical story, companies altering their play choices for different reasons. Talk about the 'Australian theatre repertoire' is a conceptual convenience. No audience attends the work of all these companies. The sense of an engulfing wave of classic adaptations is caused by a tendency to weave disparate narratives into a uniform motivation. Which is not to say changes aren't happening in our theatre, only that we will not find them at the level of statistical aggregation.

Turning back to the graphs for specific detail reveals more interesting insights. Firstly, the third data series on all of them is minimal, ranging from 2% at Playbox/

Malthouse to 7% at the MTC. No Australian company stages a significant number of Australian classics (a contrast to comparable UK companies where UK classics can be up to a third of repertoire).[9] Secondly, the first data series on the All Companies graph is not voluminous either, and falls below the average of 19% in four out of the last five years. For state theatres especially and for second-tier companies increasingly, a major portion of their Australian drama segment is made up of non-premieres, staging plays that have been staged before, in tours, co-productions or immediate revivals. It is provocative to say that this masks a problem, but it is revealing that only a small number of Australian plays receive a proportionally large number of productions, while even fewer enter the cultural memory as Australian classics. A list of programmed playwrights adds further nuance. 38 playwrights of whatever nationality (those with 10+ shows to their name) out of 761 are responsible for 711 production events (33% of the data set). Of these 38, 17 are Australian. Only five of the latter begin their mainstream careers after 1990 (Joanna Murray-Smith, Tony McNamara, Guy Rundle, Tom Wright and Matt Cameron) and only one after 2000 (Lally Katz). Five (David Williamson, Joanna Murray Smith, Louis Nowra, Michael Gow and Nick Enright) are responsible for 270 production events—around 13% of all plays produced and a whopping 24% of the Australian drama category. The majority of Australian playwrights (213) receive one or two productions.

A not dissimilar story is told by overseas classics.

Unsurprisingly, Shakespeare tops the list with 95 distinct events (a number that would be higher if the Bell Shakespeare Company were included). Within the top 38 playwrights, nine classic authors are responsible for 355 productions—17% of all plays produced and a staggering 69% of the overseas classics category. This is a narrow pool of authors, and switching from playwrights to play scripts the aperture gets narrower. 170 productions—just under half—are of 25 plays. Favourites include *Hamlet* (11 productions), *The Crucible* (9), *A Streetcar Named Desire* (6), *Uncle Vanya* (6), *Waiting for Godot* (6), *Hedda Gabler* (5), and *The Cherry Orchard* (5). Rarely produced are dramatists such as Shaw, Lope de Vega, Racine, Marlowe, Sheridan and Strindberg (only one staging of *A Dream Play*, arguably his masterpiece, and no production at all of *A Ghost Sonata*).

Ultimately, the best way to understand repertoire statistics is to read them against actual seasons. This is a laborious process and involves a degree of interpretive subjectivity. By way of example, we might look at the STC from 2007 to 2013, some 375 distinct production events. Australian plays form 45% of the repertoire (170 shows), classics 27% (102 shows) and overseas drama 28% (103 shows). But this uses a generous definition of 'Australian play' and includes all Wharf revues. A good proportion are studio productions (at Wharf 2); only a few are at larger venues (Wharf 1, the Drama Theatre, the Sydney Theatre). Of the latter, a number are clearly buy-ins (*The Narcissist, Poor Boy, When the Rain Stops Falling),* which leaves a smaller number of pure premieres: *Riflemind, The Pig Iron People, Embers, Australia Day, The Secret River, Fury*. Really, it is the international work that snares the eye: *The Women of Troy, The Wars of the Roses, A Streetcar Named Desire, Long Day's Journey into Night, Uncle Vanya, Big and Little, The Maids, Waiting for Godot*. These are invariably in larger theatres and have high media profiles. They are warmly, even rapturously received, a contrast with the Australian work that usually attracts more mixed reviews (*Secret River* is an exception). There is a high gloss quality to these seasons that reflects the spirit of the company during the period: stylish, intelligent, theatrically assured—in a word, *classic*.

—

Putting all this together we get the following picture: a sector that stages a modest (and waning) number of Australian drama premieres, mainly in its smaller theatres; that prefers the work of a small number of Australian playwrights but rarely revives this after its first seasons. Though its classic drama category has not increased numerically it has probably increased in profile, and reflects a few chosen authors, and a few plays by those authors, produced obsessively over and over again. With both Australian and classic adaptations, therefore, surface diversity hides troubling bottlenecks. Different companies package the reality in different ways, but do not fundamentally transform it. The sector's commitments are real but skew towards caution (increasingly true of second-tier companies as well as state theatres). It is manifestly failing to convert younger Australian playwrights into regular repertoire names and is largely indifferent to the revival of its own classic play scripts, two neglected areas of programming. It is a conservative repertoire, one could argue, risk-averse or attuned only to certain kinds of risks. And from a literary view there aren't many signs it is expanding in scope or depth.

It is this underlying restriction that is the real pain of the adaptations debate, a sense of a door closing for living Australian playwrights and, if they were able to complain about it, for dead ones too.

1. The Adaptive Mentality

In the sixteenth century the Danish nobleman Tycho Brahe developed a geo-heliocentric theory of the solar system where the sun and the planets had radically different orbits from the earth's. A poor model of astronomy, it is a good one of post-colonial reality. Australian theatre operates one remove from a constellation of inherently more powerful cultural entities. While we look to the world, the world does not look to us and this prompts tastes we imagine are cosmopolitan and discriminating but which can look thin and idiosyncratic. Donald Horne in *The Education of Young Donald* identifies an incessant swinging between nationalism and internationalism in the Australian public mind,[10] something John McCallum also picks up in *Belonging: Australian Playwriting in the Twentieth Century.*[11] James Curran, Canberra staffer and author, notes 'the semantic and ideological confusion which beset[s] those attempting to explain the concepts of nationalism and imperialism in British settlement colonies'.[12] The comedian Carl Barron jokes that Australians answer every question in the negative ('how you doing?'/'not bad'). Australian theatre offers a point of rebuff, defining itself against a world it both aspires to and rejects. Compounding with an historical amnesia, a toxic version of the same virus, the language of national cohesion is replaced by a set of anxious, unstable niche consciousnesses that exist side by side without interacting much.

Defining Australian theatre is not a simple matter, therefore, and the positions available for affirmation can feel a little crass. Both the 'new nationalism' of the Whitlam period that fuelled the growth of the art form in the 1970s, and the unctuous, colours-of-Benetton globalism underwriting it now are partial rhetorics that do not account for its complex ambitions and fragility. What is clear is that an 'adaptive mentality' has been part of the sector's operation right from the start. How did this come about? In the beginning, as a British colony Australia looked to Britain for its cultural norms and values. Later, however, this relationship became more systematic and coercive. I will briefly unpack this history to show that there is nothing new in the current adaptations debate; rather the opposite: that a long-term problem has raised its head again and will continue to do so until such time as it is properly confronted.

—

In 1874, J. C. Williamson, a middle-ranking American actor with a pretty wife and the rights to a pot-boiler of a play—the aptly titled *Struck Oil*—arrived in Australia. Thereafter he built the largest and most successful empire in the history of modern theatre. Until it closed its door in 1976, JCW, or 'the Firm' as it was known, oversaw professional performing arts production in

Australia according to its own corporatized, commercialized views and values. It built or refurbished a chain of notable venues and developed considerable expertise in touring a vast continent and making a profit out of it. In its heyday, before the advent of cinema chipped away at its audience base, it had up to fifteen companies on the road. It produced drama, dance, opera, music and pantomimes—huge, end-of-year spectaculars that were much anticipated—and had interests in London, New York, New Zealand and South Africa. It survived two depressions, two world wars, numerous splits between its partners, and the death of J. C, Williamson himself in 1913. It was the dominant force in our theatre for eighty years and determined, in a practical, day-to-day way, which shows Australians would see, for how long and where. Its seasons were a matter of public scrutiny and the Firm's directors did not mind discussing the thinking behind them. At its most basic this involved:

1. identifying an appropriate foreign work (whether classic or contemporary);
2. tailoring it to local sensibilities;
3. casting overseas stars and Australian supporting actors; and
4. producing it to a high technical standard, with state-of-the-art costumes and scenic effects.

Here is George Tallis, J.C. Williamson's business manager, explaining the Firm's approach to one of its most successful pantomimes:

> Mother Goose *was written by Mr J. Hickory Wood and ran at Drury Lane and at Manchester. As soon as the script arrived here it was localised, all the foreign jokes being lifted out and replaced by local ones. [...] The script ready, Mr Williamson called the heads of departments together and scene after scene was thoroughly discussed and mapped out. Then the whole thing was prepared in miniature. The scene artists draw to scale tiny models of the scenes from which the property master, the mechanists, carpenters and painters make the fairy palaces, the marvellous forests and the thundering waterfalls.[...] Next comes the cast. Mr Williamson's agents secure the necessary talent from abroad, England and America being scoured for specialists, many of whom have to be engaged a long time ahead. Quite six months before the curtain goes up on the first performance the work of selection of the local talent begins in all parts of Australia.[...] The difficulties encountered in obtaining just the right class of material may be gauged from the fact that for every ten finally selected, a thousand have been tried.*[13]

This is the adaptive mentality in action and it was, right from the start, extraordinarily successful. Imagine a European theatre with no Chekhov, Ibsen, Strindberg or Shaw; no Stanislavski, Brahm, Antoine or Reinhardt; in which the Abbey Theatre was never founded and the Royal Court experiments of Shaw and Granville-Baker did not change the face of British drama. In short, imagine a theatre in which the outlook of the nineteenth century actor-manager determined its possibilities into the twentieth. This was Australian theatre until 1950. Yet it would be wrong to think of the Firm's directors as cynical or unintelligent. They were interested in the latest staging innovations and trawled overseas markets endlessly for shows to bring back home. Williamson was a gifted stage manager, Tallis a film and radio enthusiast, interests that saved the company after 'the talkies' eviscerated the theatre market in the 1920s. The Firm was a work of business genius, a high-functioning mechanism for turning puddles of potential patrons scattered through a vast geography into a reliable audience cohort, a logic of taste. Tallis was the 'ideal' theatrical manager, 'cautious, bland, reticent, retiring'.[14] The Tait brothers whose music business allied with JCW in 1920 were driven by the same entrepreneurial ethos. 'Theatrically brilliant and dramatically inert' is a not inaccurate summary of the Firm's repertoire, which relied heavily on West End and Broadway comedies and musical comedies, with a leavening of classic revivals (mainly Shakespeare).

> *[Australian audiences] are most difficult to please, for the reason that they have been accustomed to nothing but the best. Almost every play is tried in London or New York before it is staged here, and you never see the failures. You get scenery and costumes as good as London's, and you get the*

> *most attractive plays. So audiences have naturally a high standard, and when a manager falls below that standard they are apt to complain.* (J. C. Williamson's Life-Story Told in his Own Words) [15]

Thus J.C. Williamson's established a framework of expectation around Australian theatre based on overseas endorsement, star billing, technical excellence and scenic display. It married this to a business model attuned to the market demands of its era—to audiences who wanted to feel they were worthy of the Empire's finest and that no effort was being spared to ensure that they got it.

After Williamson's death, the Tait brothers sparred with Tallis for control of the Firm's future. Live theatre was heading out of its Victorian heyday, and faced rising costs and falling revenues. So the brothers were open to different styles of programming. In 1927 they built Melbourne's Comedy Theatre, a venue of 1,200 seats, installing the best interpretive director of the day, Gregan McMahon, to provide work 'of subtler sensibilities and emotional capacities'.[16]

Early attempts to build a repertoire

The Firm's ascendancy excluded two zones of theatrical activity: overseas progressive plays and Australian drama. The first is best represented by McMahon's regime at the Melbourne Repertory Theatre and its

Sydney equivalent, the second by the playwrights' cluster around the Pioneer Players. During the inter-war years these two programming seams made strong efforts to find backers and publics. They failed. McMahon was neutralised by soft-cop recuperation (his openings were high-end society occasions and his largely amateur casts often contained prominent socialites as well), while the Pioneer Players were killed off by neglect. Writing in 1970, Dennis Douglas and Margery Morgan chart in detail McMahon's struggles in 'a small, isolated and economically vulnerable post-colonial community whose communications media were geared more and more to providing outlets for the products of foreign-owned entertainment industries'.[17] He achieved much of which the Firm was constitutionally incapable: productions of Shaw, Strindberg, Ibsen, Pirandello, Galsworthy and O'Neill. But his program was limited by what the JCW directors would allow and a nascent commitment to Australian drama was stymied at every point. There is something quintessentially self-defeating about the Firm's failure to produce Katharine Susannah Prichard's *Brumby Innes* in 1927, for example, despite its prize-winning status and the determination of both McMahon and Louis Esson to see it staged. At least McMahon was regularly employed (though he accumulated no wealth; towards the end, kind Melbourne ladies had to bring him meals). The Pioneer Players managed only three intrepid years of stuttering effort and had to be entirely self-supporting. In his biography of Louis and Hilda Esson, Peter Fitzpatrick notes that a season of plays by Prichard, Vance Palmer and Esson in 1923 attracted a lone, two-paragraph, unsigned review in the Melbourne *Herald:*

> *The first describes the evening warmly but without specific reference to anything that had taken place, and the second lists some of those in attendance. The 'review' is so blandly general it might almost have come from a bluffer's handbook [...] No plays, playwrights or participants are named.*[18]

Thus two things were split that belonged together: the directing skill and the playwriting talent. McMahon drifted away from Australian drama, and Prichard, Palmer and Esson remained un-staged. Australian audiences, habituated to a flow of overseas hits, developed little notion of what was involved in creating, as opposed to transplanting, stage work. No wonder the New Wave took its historical cue from vaudeville. By the middle of the twentieth century it was the only Australian theatre left worthy of the name.

It may seem comforting, albeit ironic, that the works McMahon premiered are the ones we regard as classics today, while the Pioneer Players are acknowledged as the womb of Australian drama. This misses the essence of the struggle. It was not just about plays but about programming sensibility. It was about *currency vs. cachet,* with the Firm backing projects only while they offered the possibility of audience acclaim, while that audience reflected 'a habit of deference, even a servility of soul, incident to the whole system'.[19] The relationship between Australian and overseas drama was deeply skewed. Whatever strengths the former might possess, it was never going to demonstrate those qualities of imperial validation that made it acceptable to a *gourmand* vision of culture. The question is whether Australia exhibits this habit of deference still or, more pointedly, whether our theatre programming does. In the eighty years since those wobbly Pioneer Players seasons, Prichard, Palmer and Esson have received less than thirty professional productions of their plays.

> *For most of our history it has been easier for foreign playwrights to find a place in our repertoire than Australian ones. This was the result not of a young country hesitantly feeling its way to theatrical confidence but the opposite: of a sector that grew too rapidly, too successfully and with too much vertical and horizontal integration; an industry that grew with its heart outside its body, self-estranged and self-displaced; a nation's theatre with a nation's drama excluded.*

—

It was politics that saved the day. In the run up to World War II a new intensity of feeling, exemplified by the New Theatre movement, swept the sector, personifying a different style of art form commitment. During the war, the difficulty of securing rights to overseas play scripts led to a more positive attitude to Australian drama. Public debate coalesced around the need for a National Theatre. Discussion of this began in the 1920s. By 1945 it was part of Labor's legislative program. There was talk of a cultural council, and drama's role in showing a working-class population how to be good citizens. What form should a national theatre take, though? Should it be a company or a body of plays? This was the McMahon/Pioneer Players split all over again and had it been faced at this juncture the history of Australian theatre would be very different. As it was, the main supporter of the new cultural agenda, Ben Chifley, decided it was unaffordable. In 1949 Labor lost power and dreams of a national theatre evaporated in a snap-back to British loyalties. When in 1954 the Governor of the Commonwealth Bank, H. C. 'Nugget' Coombs, persuaded the new Liberal Prime Minister Robert Menzies to set up an arts funding body, its name declared a mental reversion: the Australian Elizabethan Theatre Trust. It was poorly supported, incessantly fought over and plagued by the same top end of town dilettantism that had been the bane of McMahon's life.

Yet the adaptive mentality was now out in the open. In 1950, A. A. Phillips published three influential *Meanjin* articles skewering what he called Australia's 'cultural cringe'. He observed that,

> *Australia is an English colony. Its cultural pattern is based on that fact of history or, more precisely, on that pair of facts [...] This umbilical connection,*

> *incident to our colonial situation, has affected each stage of our literary development, although it has affected each stage differently.*[20]

Phillips did not assert that the Australian sensibility was *better* than the English one, only that it required a different approach to achieve its creative potential. His argument was prescient. In June, 1955 a young Union Theatre Repertory Company (later the Melbourne Theatre Company) opened Ray Lawler's *Summer of the Seventeenth Doll* to a jubilant reception. Frank Tait was in the house and refused to transfer the show. But the Trust toured it around Australia anyway, and Laurence Olivier brought it to London. A new era of effort, if not achievement, began.

A cultural conversation

If all this history is recalled when considering Australian theatre in the 1970s, certain unhelpful beliefs that have attached to it shake themselves loose. The New Wave was never spam-in-a-can nationalism, a one-eyed projection of Australian styles and values. New Wave artists neither rejected overseas drama nor slavishly imitated it. They used it as a literary resource and an intellectual framework, creating a body of work that involved a striking trade-off between past and present, international and Australian—an 'equal conversation' between converging legacies. That these remarkable plays, and the men and women behind them, should be considered narrowly nationalistic is a profound mistake. The New Wave was defined by its broad-church cultural openness which included, for the first time, openness to the products of Australia's own imagination.[21]

A good example is Nimrod Theatre's production of *The Venetian Twins,* staged at the Sydney Opera House in 1979. In 2007, I spent three months examining the archives of this play, teasing out the relationship between the original author, Carlo Goldoni, and his Australian adaptors, Nick Enright and Terence Clarke.[22] The draft scripts exhibit many features of the New Wave's syncretic imagination. Enright was both a skilled adaptor and an original playwright. Indeed, the two aspects of his authorial persona are incomprehensible without each other. Adapting *The Venetian Twins* was not a *schtick*—something he did with no goal in mind other than professional success—but a task of reciprocal cultural exchange. This takes on more meaning when we realise Goldoni was engaged in a similar project, bringing together Italy's commedia dell'arte and classically-based Erudite drama in a new theatrical fusion. It is Enright's and Clarke's understanding of Goldoni's humanist values that underpins their adaptation. What looks on the surface to be a wholly Australianised text, delivered in the vernacular and decorated with vaudeville touches, is a brilliant reinterpretation of Goldoni's rhetorical tropes and devices. The New Wave treated drama from Sophocles to Stoppard as its own backyard, unselfconsciously raiding it for inspiration and working methods. In this it behaved in the opposite way to J. C.

Williamson, favouring currency over cachet. It was an active processing of Australia's dual cultural legacy, a discovery of the new, and the new in the old, in a spirit of voracious dramatic inquiry. I'll never forget the moment when, pouring over the prompt copy I realised I was listening to a cultural conversation; that Enright and Clarke were exploring, not exploiting, their source text. *The Venetian Twins* represents a new class of authorship: both an overseas classic *and* an Australian play.

In the 1980s, this cultural processing became more sophisticated but also drew fire from a by-now significant cohort of Australian playwrights. The story is a complicated one but can be summed up in this way: Australian drama became respectable. It acquired a predictability of feature, theme and tone. Its national imaging became self-conscious. Some playwrights, like Stephen Sewell and Louis Nowra, started calling themselves 'internationalists' wanting to get away from a category they felt had become restrictive. This tension can be seen in the passing of the Australian Performing Group in 1981 and the rise of its successor, the Australian Nouveau Theatre (Anthill), founded by Jean-Pierre Mignon and Bruce Keller. Anthill's history is significant because of the battles it fought with both the profession and the funding bodies to have its adaptations of Molière, Chekhov and Beckett counted as Australian work. In 2009–10 I interviewed key members of the company, which had collapsed in acrimonious circumstances in 1994, and examined its Australia Council files. Over thirteen years it developed a sophisticated defence of its program and it is here that the contemporary debate over classic adaptations really begins. Three aspects of Anthill's approach are significant, however. First, it involved Australian writers, though this group included dramaturgs and translators. Second, the ethic of collective collaboration was strong, especially in the years when the company maintained a permanent acting ensemble (1983 and 1987). Third, Mignon's vision was anchored in a pronounced respect for his source texts. This is something he had in common with New Wave directors like Rex Cramphorn, whose patience with textual interpretation was legendary. Again and again Mignon made it clear that any erstwhile experimentalism in his productions stemmed from a strong, even exclusive, concern with the needs of his play script. It is as false to see Anthill's repertoire as conservatively classicist as it is to see the New Wave as chauvinistic. It was another productive response to Australia's dual cultural legacy.

During the 1990s, the shape of the industry changed again and new problems came to the surface. It is important not to idealise the 1970s and 1980s as a time of perfect balance between tradition and innovation, the local and the overseas. Nevertheless, in the wake of wholesale structural reform, most particularly the establishment of a Major Organisations Board by the Australia Council, there are signs that a degree of sectoral cohesion, if not autonomy, was lost. Medium-sized companies of the APG and Anthill variety, the engine rooms of repertoire reform in previous decades, reduced in number. Those that survived had very different programs. Anthill is a good example, this time in a contrast with Playbox (later Malthouse) Theatre. Until 1987, both are mixed business houses, staging work of different national and historical origins. After 1990, Anthill became a near-exclusive purveyor of classic drama, Playbox a producer of Australian plays. The McMahon/Pioneer Players split again! Around this old division a new set of industrial tensions can be seen. Directors become ascendant figures, lodestones of professional and media adulation. Directors had been important before this but in the 1990s a new insistence grows that they are the primary artists in the theatre-making process. The outstanding individual replaces the cohesive group as theatre's main delivery mechanism. (Barry Kosky's rapid ascent is a good example of this, as is the fate of his short-lived company, Gilgul Theatre).

These three factors—the decline of medium-sized theatre companies, repertoire polarisation, and the valorisation of the director—put under renewed pressure the 'equal conversation' achieved by New Wave artists in respect of Australia's dual cultural legacy. They opened up gaps in the repertoire around which a new politics of programming has grown. It is well to remember Phillips' warning that Australia's colonial legacy affects each stage of its cultural evolution differently. The expansion of national and overseas touring, the rise of international arts festivals and the development of cross-media performance means that Australian theatre today faces complex economic and artistic challenges.

The response of practitioners appears conflicted. On the one hand, there are opportunities, both at an individual and a professional level, a new positioning of Australia in the world and a transcendence of the geo-heliocentric cultural universe. On the other, there is fear about what could be lost. Given that the country laboured for so long under a louring horizon of colonial disempowerment, this fear is well founded. In the recent leadership change that has swept over Australian theatre what has been preserved or improved? This is a legitimate question and applies particularly to the repertoire. Play scripts *en masse* condition how a country thinks its own capacities, supplying a steady drip of images, stories and moments that make up what historian John Stone calls our 'social imaginary'. However peripheral they may be individually, as a job lot they are intensely representative, a slice of the public mind. Changes in theatre programming have been an indicator of national sensibility since Federation. Whatever artistic qualities classic adaptations embody, choice of their production is not, nor can ever be, a politically neutral act.

2. How Drama Works

This section briefly discusses the dramaturgical aspects of play scripts. Obviously, there is considerable variety in the field, a great number of scripts and an even greater number of potential scripts. Nevertheless, a few basic principles underlie drama *qua* drama and while they are not absolute they promote consistent traits. These involve not its artistic forms but its cognitive functioning, the way it unfolds over time. All plays must begin, for example, and be seen to begin; and be seen to begin by enough people to constitute a beginning in a collective sense. A play script is a device for turning information into experience. It processes not bytes of data or electrical impulses but human responses, prompting certain thoughts and feelings. Theatre is one of what might be called the *behavioural arts,* where acquired discipline and skill merge with given personality and presence. A zone of cognitive indeterminacy—neither purely real nor purely fictional—allows a contingent reality to unfold in the participating mind. This is theatre's 'magic if', at once celebrated and decried. It arises from our ability as human beings to engage in extended imaginative sequencing. The play script takes root here, allowing it extension and public power.

Talking in this way narrows the distance between

new play scripts and classic adaptations, since they also must manage the demands of the live stage, which stem from this unavoidable premise: time is short! At the same time it highlights their difference as repertoire choices. As a script is tested against its public meaning, its birth as a literary object is one point along a curve of development that sees it shaped by all the artists who commit to it. This process is the confronting edge of new play development, a chaotic, uneasy procedure that has everyone, including the writer, working in the dark until the moment it achieves final stage form.

Just for fun, let's imagine the life of a play in the same way that Stephen Hawking imagined the life of the universe: as a series of moments along a temporal continuum that creates not just a world but everything imaginable within it. A play is a complete set of possibilities. It is sufficient unto itself, like a human life. It is not an instrument, a tool, though it may be used as such (this is an *application* of drama, not an essential function, unlike a screwdriver or a washing machine, whose use defines their existence). On the deepest level, drama just *is* and the profound problems of its creation start here. Scripts have basic natures that make demands on all associated artists, though playwrights might maintain primary control over their literary evolution.

At every point along the development curve adapted play scripts offer easier choices than new ones. This is a provocative claim and can be disputed in individual cases (*some* problems in adaptation are more difficult than *some* problems in new script development). But it is generally true, and flows both from the generative challenges of new writing and from the issue of truth-to-nature, of having to discover, not simply transpose, a dramatic potentiality. It makes new script development a singular and forensic activity. It also makes it risky. Even when artists are of high repute the things that can go wrong are myriad. Great playwrights, one can't help but notice, write only a small number of great plays (how many of Shakespeare's thirty-six are really that good?). By contrast, adaptations fail in one way only: in the process of adaptation. Having their essential nature fixed beforehand *pace* Westwood, straightens the path of their development.

The main contrast between new drama and adaptations, however, lies not in the ways they fail but in the ways they succeed. The temporal limits of the live stage makes the theatre tyrannous, insisting that what works, works, and what doesn't, doesn't. If this remained uncontested, drama would not change much. But clearly it does. New scripts mount a challenge to the parameters of the art form, reaching out to confirm, confront or subvert the expectations surrounding it at any one time. This has led to some feisty face-offs. Think of Walter Kerr's famously dismissive review of *Waiting for Godot,* as 'a play in which nothing happens, twice'; or the remark made of the late critic Harry Kippax, that he spent so long waiting for an Australian drama to arrive he failed to recognize it when it finally came. Scripts manage expectations but expectations need to change.

Adaptations do this rarely, however, because the first

goal of the adaptive mentality is to meet them. Only with difficulty does it produce works that alter the purpose of theatre, such reforms being, as Raymond Williams says, 'the real history of art'.[23] Again this can be challenged in individual instances but is generally true. For the adaptive mentality, present expectations are the measure of failure and success. New scripts, by contrast, succeed or not via the realization of their own natures. Success is consequent to other foundational goals. Again, this has led to some significant shake-ups. Left to its own devices, commedia dell'arte changed little in two centuries, recycling stock characters and stories in a closed circle of cultural endorsement. In the space of ten years Goldoni kicked it into a new orbit of expression. Sometimes his work met expectations, sometimes it did not; sometimes it changed them altogether. This is why repertoire balance is so important. *Where classic adaptations dominate, capacity for risk diminishes; where they are excluded, they are lost as a historical resource. The two have an on-going relationship, but distinct servicing needs.*

How do the two types of script unfold at the level of cognitive structure? Plays have a number of beginnings, of which their first appearance on stage is by no means the most important. Expectations precede experience, and in theatre these are provided by the cultural context. There is no equivalent of Hawking's Big Bang, T_0, a non-time of pure potential; but the moment before a new play begins is probably the closest. Those few seconds are for me the most precious. The house is quiet, the production is yet to begin. It is an instant of rest that holds within it a journey of discovery undertaken by audience and artists alike. The script is present but not present. It is holding its breath. For classic adaptations it is different. A world has already been announced and comparative judgments are in train. The question is not 'what will happen next?' but 'what will be made of what happened then?'

Next comes a period that for most of the audience will be one of comprehension and information uptake. T_1 —T_x is a sequence that bears a preparatory relationship to the action that comes thereafter, fixing the tone, style and scope of the play in a larger sense. A literary critic would say it sketches the 'gesture of the poem', Stanislavski the 'super objective'. At any rate a *big thing* is indicated (absence of a big thing *á la* Beckett becoming the big thing itself) and an amount of data is tipped into it. With dialogue-driven scripts it is a time of exposition and character establishment. But even in shows that eschew conventional features there is still this foundational period. Before a drama can be judged, audiences must make sense of it, and making sense of what's in front of them remains their primary task throughout the entire theatre experience.

How long does T_1—T_x last? When does an audience move from the beginning of a play to its middle, from passive information gathering to thinking for themselves? Asking this aloud one day a stage manager of my acquaintance replied, half-jokingly, 'the thirty-third minute'. T_x is probably not susceptible to such exact prescription but obviously happens at some point *in* the drama. It is the first 'turn' in a script's cognitive development, and may be marked by Aristotle-type narrative revelation but equally may not be. In Ray Lawler's *Summer of the Seventeenth Doll*, *Tx* comes decisively when we learn of Roo's decision to work over the winter lay-off (announcing the drama as a parable of tragic decline). In Andrew Bovell's *Speaking in Tongues*, it arrives incrementally as we realise the two couples engaged in simultaneous infidelities are not in sync (announcing the drama as an investigation of moral choice). In *Waiting for Godot*, the moment passes without narrative mark at all, as befits a drama concerned with the absence of a supervening deity. And so on. It can be interesting, when watching a play, to note the *Tx* moment. Surprisingly often it is close to that thirty-third minute.

The first turn is something plays usually accomplish if they make it to production. However, new scripts and classic adaptations achieve the moment in different ways. For the former, *Tx* is always a surprise, for the latter never a surprise. This is a *sui generis* distinction: even when we are personally ignorant of an adaptation's subject matter, *Tx* is still defined by the assumption of public knowledge that accompanies the self-conscious notion of classic revival. For new scripts it is the opposite. Even if details about a new play have been leaked, or are the result of extensive previewing, an assumption of public ignorance underwrites their presentation. There is no cultural doubling. The first turn in a new play is an advance into new territory, a declaration and a truth. The first turn in an adaptation is a return to land already held, a reclamation and a riff.

Thereafter follows an indeterminate period during which a play complicates and an audience shifts from accruing information to accruing meaning. Audiences are now very cognitively active and scripts must allow for what in effect is a whole new reception of their action. Trying to alert young playwrights to the consequences of this I talk about a '1-to-9 ratio', that for every *one* thing their play says, an audience will have *nine* thoughts of their own. I say it knowing it to be an exaggeration. Still, ask people about their experience after they have seen a show and you often get very varied responses. A successful play successfully communicates its meaning to its presumed audience; rarely will that meaning ensue in the same way for each member.

Whatever a play has to say or show, it now has opportunity to do, in the post-foundational phase of its limited on-stage existence. If it has got this far, its choices are virtually endless. When we are deep into a drama's unfolding we are connected to a web of possibilities that bears a startling similarity to the freedom of real life. This freedom brings with it both indeterminacy and risk. As a drama heads towards a climactic plateau (or a deliberate withholding of a climactic plateau), it must contend with its own formal possibilities, the audience's responses to those possibilities (also growing in freedom) and the structural need to converge and show the point of the play overall—let's call that *Ty*. This is a tricky period and in the dramaturgical literature sports the tag of 'second act problems'. *Ty* is the next 'turn' in an audience's cognitive development, marking the moment when it is able to move ahead of the action and predict its possible end. It is these gear changes that give a night in the theatre its communal flavour, its collectively adhesive quality. If brains were audible, they would be at their loudest during the second turn of a drama. Unlike the first turn, it is not a forgone conclusion and *Ty* has been witness to many plays simply falling apart when faced with its demands.

Or rather, new plays falling apart. Classics don't because the usual reason for their selection is that they contain successfully accomplished second turns. Among other things this is what makes them classics. They evolve on cue with an audience's perception of their possibilities and purpose. It is this cognitive deepening and not any structural feature that makes them inhere. An adaptation can dispense with the story, characters and dialogue of a source text and still faithfully express its quiddity, the thing that makes it 'work' on stage. Hence the lure of classic programming. The corpus of classic scripts is diverse. Their interpretation offers a good range for any moderately skilled director and cast. The ready-made quality of their connections is a disadvantage only if viewed from the position of someone trying to say something new. Classic adaptations present economical solutions to difficult dramaturgical problems and do so imaginatively, accessibly and, most important of all, reliably.

—

For a new play, by contrast, *Tx—Ty* is a terrifying stretch where the evening is won or lost in a decisive way. What do they accomplish that make them worth the struggle? Obviously a new experience is brought into the world, but also a new thought structure. We might call this an 'argument' or 'message'. It takes the shape of a persuasive point of view, a rhetorical force arising from the action regardless of genre, style or mode. If it is of a compelling kind, an authorial perspective is conveyed that can exist in no other form. Drama has a set of problems exclusive to its own representation. New play scripts are a fresh assault on these problems so what an audience gets is not just something that 'works' but a unique inter-subjective barrage of ideas.

As it heads towards its end-time (*Te)*, to exist only in the minds of the audience who later recall it, drama is not reliant on any one mode of representation. Words, physical movement and visual image all play a role in communicating meaning and can substitute for each other: a look or a gesture can say more than pages of dialogue. In the history of playwriting some periods are more loquacious than others. Over the last one hundred years the tendency in Western drama has been to replace exposition with complex image. Compare *Summer of the Seventeenth Doll* with *Speaking in Tongues.* In the *Doll* we are told many things about Roo, Barney, Olive and Pearl, the nature of their seasonal liaison, the reasons for its souring and final collapse. In *Speaking in Tongues* we learn little about the marriages of Leon and Sonja or Pete and Jane. In place of the deliberate structuring of fateful incident, there is a vertiginous sense of chance occurrence. Images do the work: two identical hotel rooms; a discarded shoe; the nighttime bush in which the stranded Valerie, a potential murder victim, frantically phones her husband, John. Drama is a matter not of what gets said but what gets understood. Plays have access to all the channels of communication that changing technologies and sensibilities make available.

Words remain a supreme conveyer of theatrical meaning, however. Their ability to furnish a world and a point of view is unmatched. While the shape of dramatic literature has changed over the centuries, its contribution is still decisive, a deep sea of possibility wherein humanity finds its face reflected and refracted. Words are the breaker of pattern *par excellence.* While other 'languages of the stage' must work within complex traditions of socialised appreciation, words, brutally or breathtakingly, insist on their own meaning. They breach our expectations and in so doing push a drama beyond where we think it will go.

For who could know, not knowing already, that Olive would refuse Roo's offer of marriage, seeing in it a betrayal of their shared dream of freedom; or that John, hearing his wife's anguished voice on the answering machine, would not, for reasons he cannot explain, pick up the phone?

3. Adapting Ourselves to Death: My Story

Working with a group of playwrights, discussing the changes in the industry we all perceived, I mention the film *Serpico* where Al Pacino, a whistle-blowing cop, explains how his colleagues will kill him. No one has to do anything, Pacino says, just not be around when needed. Absence of support is enough to end his life. 'Tell that one', say the playwrights. 'Never mind the academic arguments. Tell that one.'

—

My employment at the Melbourne Theatre Company began in February 2002 and ended in December 2007. Thereafter I remained active in theatre, directing and developing plays for a range of companies until March 2013. At that point, having opened four new plays in three years, I ground to a halt. What overcame me was not a feeling I had failed but a feeling that it did not matter whether I succeeded or not. Behind this was a sense that the problems with which my artistic trajectory was most closely associated—those of new Australian drama—were being brushed aside. This was frustrating and, I thought, self-defeating.

I had recently completed a statistical analysis of the MTC's program from 1996 to 2006, correlating productions with attendance figures to identify emergent audience trends. To my amazement I discovered that Australian work was the second highest earner in the repertoire, behind overseas contemporary plays but ahead of classics. I was not prepared for this result. Like everyone else I subscribed to the unquestioned belief that Australian drama was a laggard repertoire choice, cross-subsidised by the success of non-Australian selections. But these numbers told a different story, of classics on the way out and Australian plays performing above trend.

> *In the Playhouse Theatre, most overseas dramas achieve attendances above the median... Australian drama starts lower than the median but quickly rises above it, and stays there. Classics, however, spend most of their time below the median with the trend line only just positive. In the Fairfax Theatre, the issue is even starker: classics flat-line, while overseas and Australian drama cut through the median at the bright line that separates pre-2002 seasons from post-2002 ones. It is clear then: classics aren't appealing to theatre-goers unless other factors are positive. Every time you find a peak in classics attendances, you find star billing.*[24]

I handed my report to the MTC Board and talked

with the journalist Robin Usher about my findings. The MTC was just one company, but these were signs that Australian drama had come of age as a repertoire category and was now a reliable source of revenue and interest for artists and audiences. This should have prompted better awareness of its needs. When I realised classic adaptations were being *forced* back into the repertoire, I became infuriated. I had no bias against classic drama; the opposite: as a literary adviser I was keen to pursue breadth of program. I was conscious that writers like Ibsen had been ill-served by recent seasons and worried that the reception of new drama would be diminished if excised from a canonical context. I was also aware of the difficulty of developing new plays: the grind; the expense; the risk; the variable outcomes. It was a tough gig. But it was also part of the sector's core mission, and if there were indications that fifty years' commitment was bearing fruit, that was both interesting and important.

Australian drama in retreat

To my eyes, the return of classic adaptations to high visibility in the mainstream repertoire looked like an avoidance strategy. 2007 should have been the year Australian drama gained momentum. Instead, it lost it. Why? I recalled the setbacks I had witnessed while working at the MTC, failures that, taken together, had weakened the commitment of the sector as a whole to new drama. There are too many of these to comprehensively relate, but four examples are:

The mishandling of Hannie Rayson at the MTC. In 2003, Hannie Rayson was one of Australia's most bankable playwrights. She had written the successful comedy *Life after George* (2000) and the hugely profitable drama, *Inheritance* (2002). She was 'the jewel in the crown of Victorian theatre' with regular appearances in mainstream seasons during the 1990s. Yet by 2010, after three unsuccessful openings in a row, she was being lambasted on the front page of the *Age* and effectively set aside.[25]

The mishandling was similar in all three cases. *Two Brothers* (2004) was programmed before its second act was written, *The Glass Soldier* (2007) before its first draft was completed, and *The Swimming Club* before its narrative arc was resolved. Hannie's ear for dialogue, her great strength as a writer, remained true but her dramaturgical structuring was flawed, in each play more catastrophically than the last. In a desire to exploit one of our few broad-appeal playwrights, the MTC programmed work before it was fully developed, either because time was too short or we didn't know how—or both. The result was the demoralization of one of Australian drama's best assets, and loss of income from the potential plays she would not be encouraged to write.

The estrangement of playwrights from the Malthouse. In 1993 Aubrey Mellor took over as artistic director of Playbox. Ten years later it was clear that a model of development that had served an older generation of playwrights was failing a younger one. In 2002, I made a study of all the play development programs around the country by way of informing my own program, Hard Lines. Playbox's approach involved the wholesale commissioning of new play scripts, most of which did not go on to production. When Michael Kantor replaced Aubrey in 2005 this model was disavowed. I played a part in this by publicising the attendance figures of Playbox's recent seasons in my Platform Paper *Trapped By the Past.*

The rebranding completed, a renovated play script program should have been put in place. Instead, the repertoire coalesced around a director-led development model and Australian playwrights were neglected. Given the key role of the Playbox/Malthouse in the historical evolution of new Australian drama (one explicitly recognised in the 1999 Nugent Inquiry[26]) this was a significant loss. By the time Marion Potts became artistic director in 2010 the company had missed an important opportunity to embed new commissions, develop new authorial voices and selectively revive old ones.

The failure of Riflemind *at the STC.* After *Two Brothers,* I began taking notes on the Australian plays I saw in order to understand the dramaturgical strategies needed to improve them. I completed a detailed analysis of *The Glass Soldier* and, shortly afterwards, of *Riflemind* by Andrew Upton (2007), who was to become co-artistic director of the STC along with his partner, Cate Blanchett. In 2002, Andrew had written *The Hanging Man*, a promising drama with some structural flaws. It was propitious that such a playwright was taking the helm of Australia's premier theatre company. *Riflemind* was staged in a transition year with a high-profile director and cast, and soon transferred to London's West End. It was another promising drama with structural flaws, ones that would have been mitigated by an extended development and production approach. The media response in the UK was vitriolic. Such public failure could only be damaging to a writer, leading Andrew to disavow 'literary' values in the theatre, and perhaps his own playwriting ambitions.[27]

The failure of the Australia Council to meet the needs of mid-career playwrights. The history of the Australia Council is a complicated one. The split between the Major Organisations Unit and the Theatre Board in 1993 deprived the latter of most of its funds, while the rise and fall of the Hybrid Arts Board in 1995–96 increased the pressure to respond to non-conventional methods of theatre-making. In 1997, a program aimed at Australian playwrights and jointly run by the Literature and Theatre Boards was scrapped. After this it was easy for the needs of writers, particularly those no longer young and emergent, to be lost. It looked to me as if the Council was trying to pass the onus of playwright development onto its client companies while actioning a notion of creative innovation that excluded new stage writing. In 2009 I wrote to the then Chair of the Theatre Board raising this issue.[28] At the time, Board members were reading only *eleven pages* of submitted play scripts. This arbitrary cut off in assessment procedures summed up a failure of understanding that had been spreading since the 1990s.

When I use the word 'failure' it is with a specific aspect of programming in mind, one where playwrights take up the challenge of larger venues and audiences. For some this equated with 'selling out' to the mainstream. I took an opposite view. I valued independent theatre, of course, but saw playwright development as a sector-wide issue, a task to be shared across a range of companies and production opportunities. I organised Hard Lines around this collective conception. Each year I took on a stable of between three and five writers, supporting them through the first drafts of their scripts and related public readings. Every month we met as a group to discuss problems, experiences and opinions. The writers had tickets for all MTC shows and I explained aspects of our operation and disabused them of unwarranted notions about our audience. Almost all Hard Lines plays went on to production, including Tony Brigg's *The Sapphires,* Patricia Cornelius's *Do Not Go Gentle,* Robert Reid's *Portrait of Modern Evil* and Felix Nobis's *Boy Out of the Country.*

While they were commissioned for MTC my aim was to contribute to Australian drama more broadly, so many were staged elsewhere. It was a fun program to run and the range of authors was diverse. It included adaptors like Tom Wright, poet-playwrights such as Ben Ellis and comedy writers like Peter Houghton. I caught them at a point when they had been writing for ten years or more and were interested in targeting their output—in marrying the values of a vocation with the realities of a career. This moment is a confronting one for any artist. But it is also potentially rewarding and offers playwrights an opportunity to step out of the garret and into a world of rich cooperation. It also provides a matchless platform for *saying something,* for presenting to an informed and interested public an artwork throwing fresh light on an aspect of our collective experience. This is a significant opportunity. Anyone who has been present at a major opening of a new play will know how powerful the sense of anticipation can be. To wrestle this into unique existence is a vast but vital creative challenge. It is to 'knock on silence', to use a phrase of psychologist Rollo May, and bravely await a reply.

My aim with Hard Lines was less to supply Australian theatre with new plays than to change its erratic approach to script development. In a nutshell, I wanted the industry to move away from 'picking winners'—a mentality that had forced the errors I list above—to 'managing talent'. I felt that the axioms of play development were not well understood. The sector was awash with poor dramaturgical advice and a failure to grasp the stepped nature of the development process. Ungrounded opinions pinged about like loose shrapnel—and with a similarly harmful effect. Play script development is about knowing what you don't know and working with what must be provisional opinions until a play is staged. Too many companies were adopting a pose of false certainty, delivering shoot-from-the-lip judgements that pointed up how little they really knew about dramaturgical development.

For a country like Australia where the context for new

stage writing is minimal to begin with, this is simply not good enough. The sector has a collective responsibility to ensure playwrights of promise are handled appropriately. It isn't about the success of any one play, it is about bodies of work, and the total contribution a playwright makes over the course of their working life.

Directing for a failing market

As a director with dramaturgical skills I was in a position to stage plays I had developed myself, and from 2006 onwards increasinglyI did this. Sometimes I failed in my efforts. *The Ghost Writer* by Ross Mueller was a play that I worked on over sixteen successive drafts and produced at the Fairfax Studio in 2007. It wasn't a disaster, but it was not entirely resolved in its characterisation, and that became apparent after we opened. I remember sitting in the theatre one day when Cate and Andrew had come down from the STC to see it and thinking, 'Well, this won't persuade them to my point of view.' But even when I was successful it didn't seem to make much difference. I directed *Do Not Go Gentle* by Patricia Cornelius at fortyfivedownstairs in 2010. It won, or was short-listed for, every major playwriting award in the country. It had a high-profile cast and did 107% business. In the two years prior I approached nearly all of the major companies about the show, without result. After the fortyfive production I felt sure it would be picked up and tour the country. Yet the play was set aside. It was as if its success did not fit into some unconscious industry agenda. Patricia was devastated, I could tell, and rightly so. She had written a play of consummate skill, one that segued her authorial values with the expectations of a broader theatre-going public. The industry response to *Do Not Go Gentle...* was a disgrace and it was at that point I realised that something had gone badly wrong with our approach to Australian drama.

Around me the changes in company leadership continued to be rung through. This was a transformation I knew was coming and knew would be hard. The previous cohort had held the commanding heights of Australian theatre for the best part of twenty years but had made few attempts at succession planning. This was consistent with their dissociated attitude towards generational change, one that I had written about in a succession of articles and books.[29] It was imperative to prevent younger practitioners from adopting the same a-historical, self-absorbed outlook that put a veneer of assurance over a morass of confusion and anxiety. The ashen harvest of another failure in cohort transmission could only fuel the hyper-competitiveness afflicting the industry, what threatened to become an industry of self-display. 'Young directors want to stage classics', one artistic director said to me, 'because their work won't be confused with the playwright's'. Distance from an author's meaning seemed to be the mark of a director's talent. Whether this was good for classic drama was debatable. It was definitely bad for new drama, where authorial intention and directorial vision must be compatible if a production is to cohere as a satisfying whole.

These were not an outsider's carps, idealistic nit-picks from someone who did not know the sector faced a range of problems in a less than perfect world. Nor was the playwriting scene devoid of hope. New talent was arriving and new ways of working were being found. Some systemic failures were of long standing and not easily fixed. Yet I couldn't shake a growing feeling of dread. The glorification of youth; the limp meta-theatricality of many productions; the thin-as-tin arrogance of some practitioners; the lack of interest in the history of the art form, including, most disturbingly, the policy history in which it operated at tax-payer expense; all this suggested a scene with its fingers in its ears, whose relationship with audiences was becoming conservative, dragging it back to the *same* plays as a way of meeting (rather than challenging) communal expectations; a scene which, for all its vivacity of staging surface, was in intellectual decline, losing the capacity to make those combative contributions that were drama's singular preserve; a scene teetering on the edge of becoming a cultural bauble.

And in a way this made complete sense. In a society drowning in information, Australian theatre reinvents itself in a register of reassurance, like opera or ballet, its repertoire known and predictable. An exhausted art form for an exhausted age, glorifying in flourish, strut, tribute, spectacle, spin, self-reference, imitation; a theatre forgetting about the world even as that world forgets about theatre.

4. A New Cultural Conversation

What steps can be taken to strengthen Australia's commitment to its national drama? My argument would be to establish a national theatre along the lines of the National Theatre of Scotland (NTS), one that is non-building-based and focussed on the commissioning, development and production of new stage work through the existing theatre company network.

For those unfamiliar with the NTS model it can be briefly sketched. It was founded in 2006, after Scotland devolved from England and established its own Parliament. The new nationally-conscious government was firmly focused on Scottish culture, both as a symbol of political change and an important contributor to the country's economy. Vicky Featherstone was selected as the inaugural artistic director. A one-time literary associate at the Bush Theatre and ex-artistic director of Paines Plough, Featherstone had made a significant contribution to contemporary drama through her support of writers such as Mark Ravenhill, Sarah Kane, David Greig, Gregory Burke and Linda McLean. She had also worked in television and had a strong commitment to an inclusive, diverse, collaborative creative culture.

This was not a vision in which the playwright was suddenly back in charge. It was a harnessing of talents in a balanced approach that allowed multiple practices to thrive, across a range of different art forms. Nor was Featherstone a born-again nationalist. The NTS, she said, 'was not, nor should ever be, a jingoistic, reductive stab at defining a nation's identity through theatre. It should not, in fact, be an attempt to define anything. Instead it is the chance to throw open the doors of possibility, to encourage boldness and for audiences to benefit from where that can take us.'[30] The first show, *Home,* was a series of thematically-linked, co-productions that opened at different Scottish towns on the same night. Its best-known work is Gregory Burke's *Black Watch,* another co-production, and it has also been active in education and children's theatre.

The NTS is an example of a national theatre that isn't a cultural edifice but a strategic operating device, one that seeks to enhance the existing theatre sector rather than supplant it. Though our state companies were founded as expressions of the same idea of theatre (British repertory), each has acquired a distinct regional identity and programming sensibility. This is even truer of second-tier companies. Calls for their wholesale reform or replacement ignore the degree to which they are hard-wired into our theatrical consciousness. A National Theatre of Australia (NTA) would add capacity while leaving this organisational capital intact. It would collaborate with existing companies to identify shared goals and better achieve them. It would produce locally but think nationally, using its position to act as a super-hub for program development across the industry. What would distinguish it is the self-consciousness of its political and artistic mission: its awareness of a need to make an effort on Australia's behalf to achieve the creative autonomy our status as a nation and our history as a people demand.

An NTA could base itself in Canberra and be federally funded, thereby avoiding the perception of Sydney/Melbourne bias and the fractious politicking that comes with variable state support. It would unite three specialisms represented by three kinds of organisation. It would be partly a playwright development agency, like PlayWriting Australia or Playworks. It would be partly a producing entity, like the state theatres and second-tier companies. And it would be partly a touring intelligence, like Performing Lines and Playing Australia. Again it would not supplant these bodies but add capacity as a partner organisation drawing on their separate spheres of operation.

An NTA has been a long time coming. Despite the challenges the size of Australia presents, and the tricky issue of establishment costs and resourcing—though it could be partly based on an endowment model and operate on an investment basis as well as a subsidy one—a national theatre is the logical way of enabling Australian theatre's enhanced existence. It is not a magic bullet but a new line of attack, one that is flexible, non-threatening and effective. Its artistic brief, like all artistic briefs, would change over time. But right now its priorities should be the development and production of Australian playwrights, especially younger ones, and the revival and reinterpretation of Australian classic drama. These are the two sins of omission of our current theatre scene, and they well suit the scope of an NTA.

—

When you assess a painting, art historians advise, do not look dead centre but slightly to one side. From this standpoint the whole canvas may be properly sighted. The adaptations debate provides a similar view of Australian theatre. It provokes strong reactions not because another Chekhov in the program impugns the national imagination but because the future of the sector has arrived and we are struggling to make sense of it. Caught between the expectations of different age cohorts, saddled with infrastructure costs that eat up capital budgets, and implicated in a changing media landscape where it is increasingly one entertainment option among many, theatre's prospects hang in the balance. Within the next decade subscription audiences will dwindle significantly. Even assuming the Australia Council can continue justifying giving upwards of 70% of its annual allocation to a small number of companies, there will be unprecedented pressure on the funding dollar. Nor is it solely a matter of money. There are principles to consider as well. What future *should* Australian theatre aspire to? Australian culture generally? Theatre programming is of interest mainly to those vulnerable to its fluctuations. But the fate of Australian drama affects cognate art forms like television, film and digital media. Leadership is effective when it understands and articulates the forces driving art forms on to the next transformation. When it doesn't, important problems are banished to the corners of otherwise arcane disputes.

This essay is not about criticising the work of younger artists. Even if some adaptations are facile, there is room for experiment in theatre and adaptors are entitled to make mistakes like everybody else.

> *The problem lies not in what Australian theatre is doing, but in what it isn't, in its latest bout of self-estrangement that squeezes out Australian playwrights.*

It lies in a course of action—new play script development—that companies find unprofitable to pursue to the extent necessary. This incentive issue merges with one of fundamental value: the need to back your own drama, despite the demands and difficulties, sometimes, even, despite the results.

When a country turns its back on a major source of dramatic imagination it is not acceding to some inevitable cultural upgrade. It is letting part of its mind die, withdrawing support, interest and love in a way that becomes self-fulfilling. Fewer plays are written because fewer plays are produced. Fewer playwrights are attracted to theatre so fewer plays are written. Remuneration plummets, expectations mount, until the pressure on those who can write plays—and it takes time, talent and courage to learn to do so—becomes intolerable and they exit the profession.

The challenge for the sector today does not lie at the level of talent, which it has in abundance. It lies at the level of commitment. This commitment is the breath of a living national drama. It is this commitment that Australian theatre in all its distinctiveness, diversity and promise must not let go.

End notes

1. Lionel Trilling, *Beyond Culture: Essays on Literature and Learning.* (London: Secker and Warburg, 1966) p.174.
2. I first tackled the issue of classic adaptations in Australian theatre in an article on *Queen Lear* that appeared last year. 'Shakespeare, Classic Adaptations and the Retreat into the Theatrical'. *Australian Studies',* October, 2013 http://www.nla.gov.au/openpublish/index.php/australian-studies/article/viewFile/3145/3639.
3. Matthew Westwood, 'Standing on the Shoulders of Giants', *Australian* 7 August, 2012.
4. Laurence Venuti, *The Translator's Invisibility: A History of Translation.* (London: Routledge 2008) p.267.
5. Linda Hutcheon with Siobhan O'Flynn, *A Theory of Adaptation.* (London and New York: Routledge 2013) p.23.
6. I am grateful for the help of Jonathan Bollen in preparing these figures. In constructing the categories, I am mindful of the difficulty of their non-controversial use, and of the unavoidable jumps in inference when interpreting quantitative data in a qualitative way. Many of these problems were raised in the on-line discussion between Alison Croggon and Rosemary Neill following the article 'The Perfect Storm'. But this exchange was unfortunately heavily skewed by their opposing positions in the adaptations debate.
7. I do not pick out adaptations as a separate category but run them into adjacent categories. In this Platform Paper I am less

concerned with the number of adaptations *per se* than with the proportions of overseas and Australian drama in the national repertoire, and with the mentality behind current programming trends.

8. 'The Perfect Storm' http://www.abc.net.au/arts/blog/Alison-Croggon/playwright-versus-director-130731/. 'If we count all work authored by playwrights, including adaptations, the proportion of local playwrights on our main stages remains pretty stable over the past decade… It seems to me that reports of the death of original Australian plays are greatly exaggerated'.
9. This is particularly true of Britain's Royal National Theatre, whose artistic mandate includes exactly these kinds of revivals.
10. Donald Horne, (Ringwood, Victoria, Penguin 1965).
11. John McCallum, (Sydney: Currency Press 2009).
12. http://john.curtin.edu.au/events/speeches/curran.html
13. Michael and Joan Tallis, *The Silent Showman: Sir George Tallis, the Man Behind the World's Largest Entertainment Organisation of the 1920s.* (Kent Town, South Australia: Wakefield Press, 1999). pp.87–88.
14. Tallis p.111.
15. http://digital.slv.vic.gov.au/view/action/singleViewer.do?dvs=1392346423593~82&locale=en_US&metadata_object_ratio=10&show_metadata=true&preferred_usage_type=VIEW_MAIN&frameId=1&usePid1=true&usePid2=true p34.
16. 'Gregan McMahon and the Australian Theatre: Part III' *Komos* 3/1-4. March 1973 p.41.
17. '*Komos.* 3/1-4 March 1973 p.41.
18. Peter Fitzpaatrick, *Pioneer Players: The Lives of Louis and Hilda Esson.* (Oakleigh, Victoria: Cambridge University Press 1995) p.195.
19. 'Gregan McMahon and the Australian Theatre: Part II'. *Komos.* 2/4. March 1973 p.130.
20. *AA Phillips on the Cultural Cringe.* (Carlton, Victoria: Melbourne University Publishsing, 2006). 'The Family Relationship'. p 24
21. See Julian Meyrick, *See How It Runs.* (Sydney: Currency Press 2002) and more recently Denise Varney's *Radical Visions 1968-2008* (Amsterdam: Rodopi 2011).
22. The result of this can be found in 'Loved Every Minute of It: Nimrod, Enright's *The Venetian Twins* and the Invention of Popular Theatre' in *Nick Enright: An Actor's Playwright* ed. Anne Pender and Susan Lever. (Amsterdam: Rodopi 2008). pp.157–72
23. Raymond Williams, *What I Came to Say.*(London: Hutchison

Radius 1989). p.105

24. Julian Meyrick, 'Melbourne Theatre Company Repertoire: A Report into Trends in Play Preferences as Reflected in Attendance Data 1996–2006', unpublished report for Melbourne Theatre Company, 2007.
25. Robin Usher, 'The MTC's reliance on perennial favourites is starting to look tired'. *Age*, 9 March 2010. http://www.smh.com.au/federal-politics/society-and-culture/the-mtcs-reliance-on-perennial-favourites-is-starting-to-look-tired-20100309-pt9t.html
26. 'Securing the Future: Major Performing Arts Inquiry Final Report'. Commonwealth of Australia, 1999).
27. Andrew's attitude towards literary values in playwriting, which at times borders on disparagement, can be sampled in his 2013 Philip Parsons Memorial Lecture and in a range of press interviews, especially Helen Trinca's 'Nothing Lost in Translation of the Classics for Modern Theatre Audience', *Australian* 26 March, 2011; and Matthew Westwood's 'Another Woman on the Verge of an Essential Part of the Show', *Australian* 26 July, 2012; as well as being reflected in his remarks during the adaptation debate.
28. Letter from the author to the Chair of the Theatre Board, the Australia Council, 30 May, 2009.
29. See the conclusion to *See How it Runs*; also my last Platform Paper *Trapped By the Past: Why Our Theatre is Facing Paralysis.* Sydney, Currency House Platform Paper No.3, 2005; and most especially 'Cutting the Fringe.' *Australian Review of Books,* June, 1999.
30. Quoted in Rebecca Charlotte Robinson's 'Funding the 'Nation' in the National Theatre of Scotland'. *International Journal of Cultural Policy* 18/1, January 2012 . p.51

Readers' Forum

A response to Peter Tregear's *Enlightenment or Entitlement: Rethinking tertiary music education* (Platform Papers 37)

Dr Michael Hooper is an ARC Postdoctoral Research Fellow in Music at the University of New South Wales.

Peter Tregear opens his paper with an overarching claim: 'Music education in Australia is in crisis'. And whilst I recognise some of the problems that he cites, the extent to which one identifies these problems as crises depends on the degree to which they are a structural part of either the sector or a particular institution.

Tregear isolates some of the shared problems, many of which are a result of the flexibility in the Australian (para) academic situation: of the necessary flexibility that comes from few non-government sources of funding for music; of the few stabilizing organizations (a role elsewhere performed by orchestras, opera companies, festivals, and publishers, for example). Both are indicative of a widely-shared appetite for change that takes little notice of past practice. The era is one of fewer risks and more distributed approaches to mitigate the impacts of change.

Understandably, much of what Tregear writes is about the changes that he has made at ANU. His paper presents a vision of broad education, of online learning across old boundaries, highly networked environments and self-directed learning. It also continues to support one-to-one teaching, specialist knowledge delivered in personal response to student abilities and interests. One-to-one lessons have recently been a site of considerable discussion internationally and Tregear repeats some of these criticisms. There remains no solid foundation for a better approach (which is why it is still offered at ANU). One-to-one teaching is still the best way of achieving high standards of performance, and since Australia has an ongoing need for accomplished performers, its teaching ought to remain a vital part of the process. Since there is no perfect education method, understanding an approach's weaknesses makes an approach more, not less, useful.

The limit of Tregear's vision, or perhaps of ANU's situation, is that it is focussed on performance students, and neither composition nor musicology figure in the argument. Both have flourished in Australian universities in recent past decades. Ignoring these aspects tends to isolate 'the performance student,' when many students move fluidly across disciplines, especially as undergraduates.

In Australia almost all the (historically) performance-focussed conservatoires now operate within a university system (this took place at ANU well before the most current undergraduates were born). Given that the vestiges of Australia's conservatoires are on a trajectory of further integration within their universities, it is difficult to make international comparisons, and it is important to recognise that most of the world's best known conservatoires are in major international cities with thriving musical scenes. They employ instrumental teachers who prize part-time, flexible teaching because this helps them maintain busy performing careers. Similarly, since one learns performance by performing, ideally students are based in a locality with opportunities to perform. Ernest Llewellyn's idea of the Canberra School of Music as an Australian Juilliard was always going to be difficult to achieve without bringing New York, too.

One of the challenges for Australia is sustaining various institutions that all offer broad programs that are more-or-less populated by students who are in their home city. Too few 18-year olds move state to learn from a particular teacher, or to pursue a particular avenue of research. This problem is amplified in Canberra, which has fewer local students on which to draw, and fewer resident professional musicians to teach performance.

One of the big differences between Australia and elsewhere is the degree to which institutions are differentiated according to their particular expertise. The UK's conservatoires, for example, each have well-known specialities. And with almost all students travelling away from home to attend these institutions (indeed, throughout Europe) there is real choice about which institution one attends. The institutions work hard to differentiate themselves from others.

Tregear makes a solid case for providing those who might not become busy professional performers with a wealth of knowledge through a model that privileges intensive performance studies. There remain a good many who enter tertiary programs without delusion and for whom a specific degree need not be instrumental in securing employment. I would also suggest that there is an ethical duty to provide a rich environment for students without predetermining their career paths.

Tregear concludes with a list of suggestions for intra-institutional structural reform. I recognise many of the desirable outcomes from my own institution, such as making possible double–degrees with a wide range of disciplines.

Other items on the list make me more nervous, particularly the suggestion that 'all music schools should embrace philanthropy [...] both as insurance against further reductions in government funding in higher education, and as one powerful benchmark tool against which to measure their effectiveness in promoting their ideas and ideals to society.' (57-8) What makes me nervous is the idea of giving philanthropists—those with the financial clout—a guiding role in benchmarking ideas and ideals. What philanthropy can provide is funding for more meeting places between performers and audiences, and there is still a need for building recital halls, funding ensembles and (perhaps most of all) subsidising ticket prices. The latter is needed to combat the growing association between wealth and particular art forms.

Tregear advocates a moderate path, blending ideas from various places. It may be that the technological changes that he has outlined are more radical than they currently seem, are less instrumental, and more able to mediate against long established patterns.

If there is something approaching a crisis in 'Music education in Australia' then larger structural questions about music education remain, and the degree to which institutions specialise needs to be carefully addressed.

FORTHCOMING

PP40, August 2014
TAKE ME TO YOUR LEADER:
The dilemma of cultural leadership
Wesley Enoch

To celebrate ten years of Platform Papers, tracking the cultural thinking and opinion of the nation, our editors have invited Wesley Enoch, Director of the Queensland Theatre Company, to define what we mean by cultural leadership; and to ruminate on its importance today in building community and opening new directions. With the growth of government-led cultural leadership, he asks, have we obscured the core reasons why the arts exist? We have seen the voices of the mob, the dissenters and the rambunctious opposition slowly becoming tamed and included in a sort of official culture, he says. Government champions the arts more these days than artists do.

Enoch finds the arts community ridden with mistrust, and fearful of those who speak out. Australia, he concludes, is in great need of cultural leadership; of a fresh force to challenge thinking and gather confidence. He learnt his thirst for dissent and debate in Aboriginal community politics, he says. It gave him a thick skin and an iron jaw. But he is still standing, and defends the role of the embattled elders, custodians of our values and our history.

Copyright Information

PLATFORM PAPERS
Quarterly essays from Currency House Inc.
Founding Editor: Dr John Golder
Currency House is a not-for-profit association and resource centre advocating the role of the performing arts in public life by research, debate and publication.

Postal address: PO Box 2270, Strawberry Hills, NSW 2012, Australia
Email: info@currencyhouse.org.au Tel: (02) 9319 4953
Website: www.currencyhouse.org.au Fax: (02) 9319 3649

ISBN 978-0-9872114-9-1
ISSN 1449-583X
Typeset in Garamond
Printed by McPhersons
Production by Xou Creative
Author's photo by Christopher Deere